Poppy Love titles

Poppy Love Steps Out

Poppy Love Faces the Music

Poppy Love Rock 'n' Roll

Poppy Love Star Turn

Poppy Love In the Spotlight

Poppy Love Tango Queen

Visit Poppy Love at

www.poppylovelovestodance.com

Lancashire Library Services	
11300385 ろ	
PETERS	JF
£3.99	16-Oct-2009
SOR 11/09	

Poppy Love
Tango Queen

NATASHA MAY

illustrated by

SHELAGH McNICHOLAS

WALKER
BOOKS

*With thanks to Neil Kelly and the students of
Rubies Dance Centre
N.M.*

*With thanks to Carolyn, Julia, Kirsty and Ann at
Bell's Dance Centre
S.M.*

This is a work of fiction. Names, characters, places and incidents are
either the product of the author's imagination or, if real, are used
fictitiously. All statements, activities, stunts, descriptions, information
and material of any other kind contained herein are included for
entertainment purposes only and should not be relied on for accuracy
or replicated as they may result in injury.

First published 2009 by Walker Books Ltd
87 Vauxhall Walk, London SE11 5HJ

2 4 6 8 10 9 7 5 3 1

Text © 2009 Veronica Bennett
Illustrations © 2009 Shelagh McNicholas

The author and illustrator have asserted their moral rights
in accordance with the Copyright, Designs and Patents Act 1988

This book has been typeset in ITC Giovanni

Printed and bound in Great Britain by Clays Ltd, St Ives plc

All rights reserved. No part of this book may be reproduced,
transmitted or stored in an information retrieval system in any form
or by any means, graphic, electronic or mechanical, including
photocopying, taping and recording, without prior written
permission from the publisher.

British Library Cataloguing in Publication Data:
a catalogue record for this book is available from the British Library

ISBN 978-1-4063-2023-7

www.walker.co.uk

Contents

Tango Queen

Poppy Love loved ballroom dancing.

She and her partner, Zack Bishop, went three times a week for lessons with Miss Johnson at the Blue Horizon Dance Studios. They had already passed medal tests and done well in competitions. So well, in fact, that they had qualified to take part in the Nationwide Finals, which were held every Easter in the seaside resort of Blackpool.

Their home town, Brighton, was also a seaside resort.

"Has Blackpool got a beach and a pier, just like Brighton?" Poppy asked Miss Johnson one evening before dance class.

"Yes," replied Miss Johnson, "and the seafront's called the Golden Mile because it's all lit up. There's a famous tower, too, with a ballroom under it."

"I'll race you to the top of Blackpool Tower!" said Poppy to Zack.

"OK, but I'll win," said Zack confidently.

"You'll need all your energy for dancing," said Miss Johnson. "The standard will be very high. Everyone there has qualified in regional competitions, remember, just like you have."

Poppy and Zack hadn't forgotten. They looked at each other. "What will we do if they're all brilliant?" he asked.

"We'll just be brillianter!" answered Poppy.

Miss Johnson laughed. "Poppy's right, you know," she told Zack. "You two *will* be brilliant if you work hard."

Other children were arriving. It was the first class after the Christmas holidays, and they were all glad to see their friends again. "Happy New Year!" they said to each other. Everyone was excited about the Nationwide Finals, too.

"I'm going to have a new red dress for Blackpool," said Cora, Poppy's pretty, curly-haired friend. "With red flowers in my hair."

"Oh, that'll look lovely!" exclaimed Poppy.

Miss Johnson called to the children to

spread out and face the front, ready for the warm-up exercises they always did at the start of class. "Now," she said, "I couldn't help overhearing what Cora said to Poppy, about wearing flowers in her hair. It reminded me of the new dance we're going to learn this term."

The children were puzzled. They already knew the ten dances – five ballroom and five Latin American – required for competitions. Why did Miss Johnson want them to learn a new one, when the most important competition of all was only a few weeks away?

"Oh, no!" exclaimed Sam, who had arrived late and was scrambling into his place beside his partner, Sophie. "Isn't ten dances enough, miss?"

Miss Johnson smiled as she started the CD player. "Do any of you know which dance goes with this music?" she asked.

The children listened carefully. Poppy could hear the soft strumming of a guitar, and another instrument, perhaps a trumpet, making a sound like someone singing sadly. She had never heard the music before.

"It sounds a bit Spanish," said Sophie.

"It's for the Argentine tango," replied Miss Johnson. "You've seen that on TV, haven't you?"

The children nodded. The Argentine tango was different from the striding, head-flicking ballroom tango, and wasn't included in competitions. The dancers stood close together, turning in a small space. Poppy had always thought it looked complicated, though very beautiful.

"Argentine tango dancers often wear flowers in their hair," Miss Johnson said to Cora. "And a dress that comes to their knees. No long frilly skirt! The Argentine tango is slow, but quite difficult. I think it will be a good challenge for you."

Sam began to groan, pretending he had a pain in his stomach.

"And if you learn it properly," added their teacher, "you can do it as a show dance next month at the Worthing Dance Workout."

Sam groaned louder. Every year the Dance

Workout was held in Worthing, a smaller seaside town than Brighton. There was a children's competition, and a dance festival, and crowds of people watching.

"Sounds like fun," said Poppy. "I love doing show dances!"

"I think it sounds fun too," said Miss Johnson. "And although you've competed in bigger events, I think it will be good experience for you all before the Nationwide Finals."

"Are you joking, miss?" exclaimed Sam.

Miss Johnson smiled. Everyone knew she *wasn't* joking. "If you can do the Argentine tango, Sam," she said, "you can do any dance in the world. Now, let's begin our warm-up."

* * *

Poppy's older brother Tom was sitting on the carpet in front of the TV, playing a video game, and Poppy was lying on the sofa, trying to read a book. But she couldn't keep her mind on it.

"When do you think they'll get here?" she asked.

Tom's Spanish friend Rafael Costa and his parents, who had been having a Christmas holiday in London, were coming to stay for the weekend. Dad had gone to pick them up from Brighton station.

Tom looked at his watch. "Any minute now," he said.

Two summers ago, Rafael's school group had stayed at the Hotel Gemini, where the Love family lived. The Spanish children had come to learn English, but Rafael and Tom were soon such good friends that Tom ended up learning quite a lot of Spanish, too.

Poppy was excited to be seeing Rafael again. She remembered his honey-coloured skin and spiky black hair, and how he was always playing some game, indoors or out. He didn't sit still for one minute.

He hadn't changed. Poppy heard his feet stomping up the stairs to the Loves' flat at the top of the hotel. The door flew open, and there he stood, smiling from ear to ear. Poppy found herself being hugged tightly, not just by Rafael but by his mum and dad too. They all seemed very pleased to see her!

"Make yourselves comfortable," said Mum to the Costa family, "and I'll get us some coffee."

Rafael's dad sat beside Poppy. He looked just like his son, only taller. "Rafael tells us you are very good at dancing," he said.

Poppy felt shy. "Um … yes, I *love* dancing!"

Mrs Costa, who was dressed smartly, with her hair tied up at the back of her head, smiled kindly at Poppy. "My husband likes to do the tango," she said.

Poppy thought dark-haired, elegant Mrs Costa looked like the Spanish dancers she'd seen in pictures. "I do too!" she said.

"Back home we call my wife the tango queen," said Mr Costa.

Poppy was too shy to ask him why. But to her delight, as Mum served coffee and Rafael and Tom played video games, Mrs Costa told them.

"I am from Argentina," she explained. "As a young girl in Buenos Aires, I was always going to clubs and bars where you can dance."

"Especially the Argentine tango," added her husband, sipping his coffee.

Poppy could hardly believe her ears. What a surprise! Just as she had begun to learn the dance, a real Argentine tango dancer had arrived!

Mrs Costa looked fondly at her husband. "Roberto and I met at a tango club, you see," she explained. "But I haven't danced the Argentine tango since we got married and moved to Spain. I've probably forgotten how."

Poppy's heart beat a little faster. She was sure that Mrs Costa hadn't forgotten how to be the tango queen. And the Argentine tango was so hard to learn. What if Poppy could see Mrs Costa dance it properly, the way it was done in Buenos Aires?

Noticing that everyone had finished their coffee, Mum stood up. "Would you like to see your rooms?" she asked.

"Thank you," said Mr Costa. "Come along, Rafael."

"But I'm in the middle of this game!" protested Rafael.

"Why don't I show Raf his room when we've finished the game?" suggested Tom.

"All right," said Dad, "but don't be long."

When the grown-ups had gone Poppy sat down beside the boys. "I'd love to see your mum dance the Argentine tango, Rafael," she said.

Rafael looked doubtful. "Well…" he said, "I'll ask her if you like." He pressed the buttons on his console as fast as he could. "You're too good, Tom!" he cried. "I just lost *again*!"

"Maybe you won't need to ask her," said Poppy in a whisper, so that Tom didn't hear. "I've got an idea, but I need your help."

Rafael's dark eyes looked interested. "What are you going to do?" he whispered.

"I'll tell you in a minute," replied Poppy as she stood up. "It's all right, Tom," she said to her brother, who was still absorbed in the video game. "I'll show Rafael his room."

* * *

Poppy really liked Forrester's, Uncle Simon's restaurant – especially the dance floor at the back, where people often had so much fun dancing that they let their dinner get cold. Tonight, Uncle Simon and his staff were

making a special effort to give the Loves and
the Costas a good time.

"This is wonderful!" exclaimed Mrs Costa
as the waiters took her coat, pulled out her
chair for her and put her napkin on her lap.
"I feel like a princess!"

"Or a queen," said Rafael to Poppy under
his breath.

"Shh!" said Poppy. "It's got to be a surprise!"

Rafael pretended to zip up his lip, his eyes
sparkling. Poppy couldn't wait to put their
plan into action.

"Hello, everyone!" said Auntie Jill,
bringing the menus. She bent down
and whispered something in
Poppy's ear.

"Thanks!" said
Poppy.

They ate so much delicious food that when the waiter asked if they wanted dessert, Mr and Mrs Costa both shook their heads. "I couldn't manage another mouthful," said Mrs Costa.

"But you *must* have some famous Forrester's ice cream!" exclaimed Tom.

"Maybe we'll all feel like having ice cream if we wait a little while," suggested Dad.

Auntie Jill squeezed Poppy's hand under the table, then went to speak to the leader 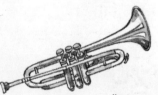 of the band. Suddenly, the trumpet music of the Argentine tango began.

"Listen to that!" exclaimed Mrs Costa, her eyes shining as she recognized the sound. "I could almost be back in Buenos Aires!"

"Come on, Poppy," said Rafael. "Want to have a try?"

Rafael said this so naturally no one would have guessed that it was planned. And no one watching them would have guessed what they were going to do.

"Just remember what I told you," said Rafael, taking Poppy's hand, "and forget everything you learned from your teacher!"

As more couples joined them on the dance floor, Poppy and Rafael began to do the Argentine tango. Poppy kept stepping on Rafael's toes. When he turned one way, she turned the other and he had to pull her back. And instead of placing her foot neatly between his feet, she missed, and kicked his ankle.

"I'm sorry!" she cried, stepping back and putting her hand over her mouth. "I'm terrible at this!"

"Watch us, then," said Mr Costa. He and his wife had appeared beside them. "This is how it's done in Argentina," he said, and he took Mrs Costa in the dance hold.

Rafael held out his hand for Poppy to slap. "Job done!" he said.

"Shh, they might hear you!" warned Poppy.

But Mr and Mrs Costa couldn't hear anything but the tango music. They swayed

to the haunting, soaring trumpet sounds and the rhythmic guitars, their cheeks touching. It was as if they were dancing in a dream.

Mrs Costa looked beautiful in her black dress and high heeled shoes, with a gold ornament in her hair. Her movements were graceful and strong. Poppy thought she did the difficult steps as well as any of the dancers she'd seen on TV.

Rafael's eyes followed his mother and father proudly. *"Tango fantástico!"* he said. "You got them to dance again, Poppy."

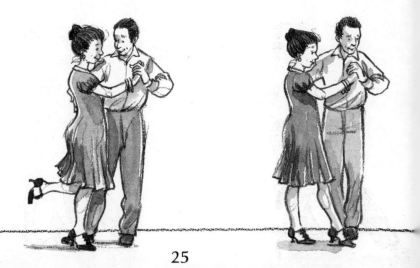

"You mean *we* did," said Poppy.

He held out his hand. "Shall we dance the tango?" he asked. "Properly, this time?"

"*Fantástico!*" exclaimed Poppy, copying the way Rafael said it. It was the first Spanish word she'd learnt.

Rafael laughed delightedly. "You're good at Spanish *speaking* as well as Spanish *dancing*," he told her. "Do you know something, Poppy? *You're* the real tango queen!"

Dragon Dance

The holidays were over. Dad went to catch his train to London with a sigh, while Tom trudged off to school with his head down. The Gemini Hotel was closed for its yearly repairs. Living in a hotel was fun when it was full of guests, but in January there was nobody there except plumbers and painters.

Poppy felt that Easter, and the Nationwide Finals, were ages and ages away.

"Why is everyone so cross at this time of year?" she asked Mum as they laid the table one dark evening.

"Not cross, really," said Mum. "It's just that it's very hard going back to work, or school, after Christmas."

"What can we do to cheer ourselves up?" asked Poppy.

Just then the door bell rang. "I'm not expecting anyone," said Mum, putting down the knives and forks and going to the door. There stood Poppy's friend Mia and her mum, both smiling big smiles.

"Hi, Mia!" cried Poppy.

"What a lovely surprise!" said Mum.

"Mia couldn't wait to tell Poppy her news," explained Mrs Porter as they all went into the sitting-room. "So we called in on our way home from gymnastics."

Mia began to jog up and
down, which she always did
when she was excited. Her
black pony-tail flipped from
side to side, and her shiny dark

eyes looked even shinier than usual. "Would
you and Zack like to be in the dragon dance,
Poppy?" she asked breathlessly.

"What dragon dance?" asked Poppy and
Mum together.

"It's for New Year," said Mrs Porter.

"But we've just *had* New Year," said Poppy,
puzzled.

"Excuse me," said Mrs Porter. "I meant
Chinese New Year, which is next month."

Mia's mum came from China. Poppy
thought she looked lovely. Her figure was

small and neat, and her hair was as smooth as jet-black silk. "The Chinese people in Brighton are planning big celebrations this year," she went on, "with Chinese food, and fireworks, and the traditional dragon dance."

A feeling of excitement started to bubble up inside Poppy. "Oh, I've seen that dance on TV!" she exclaimed. "There was a model of a dragon's head, with a long body, and people made it dance. It looked so cool!"

"It *is*!" said Mia. "It's normally only boys who hold up the poles to make the dragon dance, but because I do gymnastics, they said I could be in it, and they needed two more children, and I said I knew a boy dancer and a girl dancer, and they said that's OK." Her words were tumbling over each other in her excitement. "Do you want to do it, Poppy?"

"Yes, please!" said Poppy.

"Will Zack want to?" asked Mia.

"Let's ring him," said Mum, picking up the phone.

"There'll be an adults' dragon dance in the evening," added Mrs Porter, "but this one's for the children, in the afternoon." She smiled at Poppy. "It'll be like a party in the street," she said.

"Wow!" said Poppy. "I was just wondering what we could do to cheer ourselves up, and now I've found it!"

Poppy couldn't wait for Chinese New Year. On the first day of rehearsals, she was very excited, and also a little nervous.

"I hope we don't do something wrong," she said to Zack.

"I expect we will," he replied.

"Don't worry," said Mia. "Just follow everyone else. Oh, look, here's the dragon."

A boy came in, holding up the dragon's head. The head was painted brightly in red, green and gold. It had a wide mouth with a curly tongue inside, huge, staring eyes and pointed horns. The long body part was made of shiny material decorated with scales.

Poppy thought it was a bit scary.

The boy smiled at Mia, Poppy and Zack. "I'm the one that dances at the front," he said cheerfully. "People call me Charlie because no one can say my Chinese name."

"I'm Poppy," said Poppy. "Isn't the dragon's head heavy to hold up?"

"Not really," said Charlie. "It's only made of papier mâché."

Poppy kept thinking up questions. "Why does the dragon *dance*?" she asked. "Isn't a dragon a nasty thing, that breathes fire and eats people?"

"In some stories it is," replied Charlie. "But in Chinese stories it's friendly and brings luck, even though it's fierce and bold."

"And it flies, too," added Mia.

"So when we dance," said Charlie, "we try to make it look as if it's whirling and twisting in the air."

"Awesome!" said Zack.

The children were going to be taught how to do the dance by a man called Nick, who was the leader of the adults' dragon dance team. He looked very strong.

"We're going to make the dragon writhe like a snake, run like a rabbit, fly like a bird and swim like a fish," he said. He and Charlie, who had performed the dance before, put down the dragon and showed the children the movements. "Are you ready?"

Poppy found it difficult to see where she was going while holding up the dragon's body on a pole. And she had to keep her steps in time with all the other children in the line, or everything would go wrong.

It was a bit like running a three-legged race, but with eighteen legs! And it wasn't

so much dancing, but jogging, stopping, crouching, turning, twisting, and all the time moving the pole so that the dragon's body danced. Poppy got very hot and confused.

When Nick said they could have a ten minute break, Poppy, Zack and Mia sat down on a bench by the wall. "This isn't like any dancing I've ever done before," said Zack.

"Me too," said Mia, whose cheeks looked very pink. "It's hard, isn't it?"

Poppy knew that to learn a new dance was always hard at first, then it suddenly clicked. "Don't worry, Mia," she said. "We'll get it right in the end."

After the break, all nine children worked very hard. By the time the rehearsal was over, they had managed to make the dragon dance round the room without colliding with each other.

"Best team I've ever had!" declared Nick.

The children were very pleased. "This is fun!" Poppy said to Mia and Zack. "When's the next rehearsal?"

When Poppy woke up she looked out of her attic bedroom window. Today was the day they were to perform the dragon dance – and it was raining! Below, the roofs and streets of Brighton looked shiny and grey, and it was so cold, Poppy hoped they could still do the dance. But by lunchtime the rain had lessened. And by two o'clock, when the children had to be ready in their red and gold costumes, it had stopped altogether. As the parade began, the sky brightened up.

"I told you the dragon brings good luck!" said Mia.

The Chinese people of Brighton had spent months preparing for the parade. Mia told Poppy that the New Year celebrations went on for two weeks, ending with the dragon dance. Poppy felt very special to be chosen to be part of such an important festival. She held her pole tightly, and at the signal from Nick, she and

the other children began to do the small
running steps that made the dragon fly above
their heads.

The air was full of music. Poppy
could hear drums and flutes, and the
crashing and tinkling of instruments
she didn't know the names of.

Ahead of the dragon in the parade
there were young jugglers and
acrobats, and little girls in traditional
Chinese costume. Their complicated
headdresses looked fragile, but very heavy.
Poppy couldn't imagine being able to *walk* in
one, let alone do the careful, stately steps and
turns the girls were doing. Some children
held streamers, which made patterns as
they moved, and others carried brightly lit
lanterns painted in wonderful designs.

Poppy had never seen anything more beautiful than the Chinese New Year celebrations. Her family would be somewhere in the crowd, but she didn't have time to look for them. Before she knew it, the parade had ended in the square, and the dragon dance was underway.

Boom, boom! went the drums. Loud crashes came from the cymbals. Bells rang and whistles sounded, and Charlie began to wave the dragon's head around, dipping and rising, this way and that. The people in the crowd stared in amazement.

Off went Poppy, Zack, Mia and the others, following Charlie. The dragon flew, the golden sides of its scaly body billowing out. Then it swooped down and crawled like a snake, close to the ground, and suddenly rose again, twisting and turning as if it were alive. Above the music Poppy could hear the audience screaming with delight and applauding. This was the best fun!

It was hard work, though. When the dance was over, Poppy felt very tired, and hungry, too. She'd been too excited to eat lunch. Then suddenly, everyone appeared at once.

"That was incredible!" said Dad, bending down to hug Poppy.

"I didn't know it was going to be like this!" said Mrs Bishop, Zack's mum.

"Did you know which one was me?" Poppy asked them.

"Of course," said Uncle Simon. "We'd recognize your legs anywhere."

"I bet you didn't!" said Poppy. But she
didn't mind. The dragon dancers had to be
as invisible as possible, so that the audience
would look only at the dragon.

Mrs Porter led the way to the stalls at the
edge of the square. "This is Chinese street
food," she said. "Do you want to try some?"

"Yes, please!" said Poppy and Zack
together. "Unless…" added Zack, catching
sight of a large picture of a rat above one of
the stalls, "…it's roasted rat or something!"

Mrs Porter looked puzzled for a moment,
then she laughed. "Oh, no!" she said. "That
sign is to show that this will be the
Chinese Year of the Rat."

Poppy looked at Mia's mum in
surprise. She'd never heard of
the Year of the Rat.

"In China we name years after animals," explained Mrs Porter, "and you're said to be like the animal of the year you were born in. I was born in a rat year, so I'm a rat."

Mia came back with a cardboard plate laden with food. "Rats are supposed to be charming," she said. "And I think my mum is!"

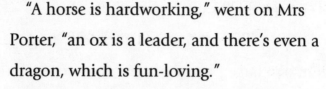

"A horse is hardworking," went on Mrs Porter, "an ox is a leader, and there's even a dragon, which is fun-loving."

Poppy was interested. "Which animal are you, Mia?" she asked.

"A pig," said Mia. "We're supposed to be good at making friends."

"And what am I?" asked Poppy. She really, really hoped that she was a dragon.

Mrs Porter studied a little calendar she kept in her purse. Then she looked at Poppy, her black eyes full of amusement. "You're the same as me!" she told Poppy. "You're a rat! So these New Year celebrations are special for both of us!"

After that, of course, Zack wanted to know what animal *he* was.

"Oh, Zack!" exclaimed Mrs Porter, looking at her calendar. "You're a dragon!"

Uncle Simon was a sheep and Auntie Jill a dog.

"You see, Simon, I should be in charge of you," Auntie Jill teased.

"You already are, aren't you?" he said.

Laughing, they all gathered round the stall, eating Chinese food and talking about Chinese things until it was dark enough for the fireworks.

"I sort of wish I was a dragon," said Poppy
sleepily on the way home. "They're fun-
loving, like Zack. But rats are charming,
which is OK."

"You'll just have to be a charming rat
that's fun-loving too," suggested Dad. "And
judging by the fun you've given all of us
today, Poppy, I don't think you'll have much
trouble with that!"

Special Sunday

It was another rainy Sunday – Poppy was
getting tired of all this rain! She was practising
dance steps alone in her bedroom. She
watched herself in the big mirror, trying to get
her arms just how Miss Johnson said they had
to look in the Argentine tango. Poppy wished
Zack was beside her. But he and his mum had
gone away for the weekend, so she had to
practise her movements on her own.

It wasn't the same as doing them in class, though. She stopped, sighed, and said to her reflection, "I'm so bored!"

She was lonely, too. Tom was doing his homework in his bedroom, Mum was working downstairs in the hotel and Dad had gone to play squash. Auntie Jill, who used to have the bedroom next to Poppy's, had moved out of the flat when she got married to Uncle Simon. Although Poppy was very happy for her, she couldn't help missing her.

If only … no, it wasn't possible. Poppy had

 been going to wish that she had a puppy. On days like today, a puppy would be the perfect companion. But Mum and Dad said it wouldn't

be fair to keep a dog in a high-up flat, alone all day and with no garden to run in.

"Poppy!" called Tom's voice outside her door. "Uncle Simon's on the phone for you!"

Poppy had been so busy dreaming that she hadn't heard the phone ring.

"Hi, Uncle Simon!" she said.

"Hello, Poppy," replied her uncle. "What are you doing this afternoon?"

"Nothing," said Poppy. "I'm bored stiff."

Uncle Simon's laugh came loudly down the phone line. "Well, how about coming round to our place to see Auntie Jill's new DVD?" he asked. "We just got the first copies yesterday."

Poppy's aunt, who used be a ballroom dancing champion, was in a DVD for teaching people how to keep fit by doing basic ballroom steps. "Oh, yes, please!" said Poppy.

"I'll just phone the hotel desk to make sure it's OK with your mum, then I'll come and pick you up. And you can stay for supper!"

"Thank you so much!" said Poppy. Her boring Sunday had disappeared. "See you later!"

Poppy changed into jeans and trainers, washed her face, cleaned her teeth and brushed her hair. The face that looked back at her from the mirror was quite different from the gloomy one she'd seen before Uncle Simon had phoned.

"That's better!" she said to herself.

She said goodbye to Tom, and went down the stairs to wait for Uncle Simon.

"Have a good time, won't you?" said Mum as they saw the car draw up. "And look at that rain!

You'd better put your hood up, love."

Poppy ran to Uncle Simon's car with her hood pulled closely around her face and her head down. So it wasn't until she opened the door that she noticed Uncle Simon wasn't alone. In the back seat, smiling a mischievous smile, sat Auntie Jill.

"Hello, Poppy!" she said. "I thought I'd come with Simon, just to get out of the house."

Poppy slid into the front seat and did up her seatbelt. "That's nice," she said, though she thought it was a bit odd. No one would go on a five-minute car ride, and back again, in the rain, just to get out of the house. And Poppy knew that the way her aunt was smiling meant she had a secret. What was she up to?

They set off, the windscreen wipers going so fast Poppy could hardly see out of the window. Then something else strange happened. Instead of driving home, Uncle Simon took a main road out of Brighton, into the countryside.

"Where are we going?" asked Poppy.

Uncle Simon just smiled, and all Auntie Jill said was, "Wait and see."

Poppy wondered what was going on. If her aunt and uncle had a surprise for her, what could it be? And why? It wasn't her birthday. It wasn't any sort of special occasion. It was just an ordinary wet Sunday.

"How's the dancing going, Poppy?" asked Auntie Jill as the car sped along country lanes between the fields.

"Oh, it's good," replied Poppy. "We're still trying to get the Argentine tango right for that dance event Miss Johnson's entered us for."

"Oh, the Worthing Dance Workout?" said Auntie Jill. "How lovely – the Argentine tango's such a beautiful dance."

"And the costume is lovely!" added Poppy excitedly. "We tried our dresses on in class yesterday. They're black and red, and they look so grown-up, and we've got black ribbons round our necks with a flower on. Miss Johnson says the ribbon's called a choker."

"Does that mean it's going to choke you, then?" joked Uncle Simon.

"Just drive!" Auntie Jill told him.

Poppy smiled, but she was thinking about something else.

"Miss Johnson says Zack and

I can win the competition in Worthing if we really try," she said to Auntie Jill. "Wouldn't it be amazing if we did? We've never won anything."

"Don't worry," said Auntie Jill. "You'll win something some day, even if it's not quite yet. You and Zack are a good partnership."

"I think so too!" agreed Poppy.

Although the rain had lessened, the car windows were still steamed up. Poppy rubbed a peephole, but it didn't help much. The countryside was just a brown and green blur as they rushed past. "*Please* tell me where we're going!" she pleaded.

"Nearly there," said Uncle Simon, turning off the road onto a bumpy track between two gateposts. "What shoes have you got on, Poppy?"

Poppy stuck her feet out. "Trainers," she
said.

"Wellies would be better," said Uncle
Simon, "but at least you haven't got your
dancing shoes on."

"That would be silly," said Poppy, though
she knew he wasn't serious. What could she
need wellies for? They must be going out in
the rain.

"If it's very muddy, you could carry Poppy,"
said Auntie Jill to Uncle Simon. "She's only
little."

"I'm not *that* little!" protested Poppy.

Then she forgot all about whether she was
little, and wellies, and everything, because
she had seen a notice that said: HILLSIDE DOG
RESCUE. "Oh!" she exclaimed, looking
from her aunt to her uncle

and back again. "Oh!" she said once more.

All three of them started laughing at once.
"That's right, Poppy!" said Uncle Simon as
he parked the car. "Come on, let's go and
choose you a puppy!"

They walked further up the track to some
kennels. "This is a rescue home," explained
Auntie Jill as they opened the gate. "They've
been looking after a dog that was abandoned
just before she gave birth to her litter. So now
they've got lots of puppies!"

A friendly teenage girl appeared. Uncle Simon and Auntie Jill had phoned to make an appointment, so she was expecting them. "I'm Lisa," she said, leading them down a corridor. She stopped and opened a door. "Here are the puppies. They're twelve weeks old."

The puppies were in a room which had a yard outside so that they could run around. Some of them were curled up asleep, but some pricked up their ears and bounded towards Poppy and the others, eager to play. The mother dog raised her head, decided that nobody was going to hurt her babies, and went back to sleep.

Poppy was so happy she could hardly
breathe. "Can I really choose one?" she asked
her aunt and uncle.

"Of course," said Auntie Jill. "We didn't
forget the promise we made, even though
you never reminded us!"

"Any one I want?" asked Poppy, still
unable to believe it.

"Any one you want," said Uncle Simon.

"Oh, I love them all!" cried Poppy.

She sat down on the floor. The puppies
climbed over her knees and tried to lick her
face. Even the ones who had
been asleep joined in.

They were dark brown puppies, some with white markings. They were all beautiful, with black eyes that looked happy and sad at the same time, busy little tails and big paws.

One of them was a bit smaller than the others. It was lively enough, but kept getting pushed out of the way by its bigger brothers and sisters. The puppy had white markings on its face, exactly like Poppy's soft toy puppy, Lucky.

"Is that one a boy or a girl?" she asked.

"That's a boy," Lisa told her.

Poppy picked up the little boy puppy and cradled him under her chin. The top of his head felt like velvet.

57

"Can I have this one?" she asked. "I think I love him the best!"

"Well, that didn't take long," said Uncle Simon. "Are you sure, Poppy?"

"Yes," said Poppy. "He looks like Lucky, so I'm going to name him Lucky."

While Uncle Simon was talking to Lisa about the puppy, Auntie Jill put her arm round Poppy's shoulders. "You remember, don't you," she said, "that the real Lucky is going to live at our house, though he'll belong to you. You're OK with that, aren't you?"

Poppy nodded. It was a pity, but it had been agreed with Mum and Dad. Having a part-time puppy was a lot better than having no puppy at all. "That's why I still want the old Lucky," she told her aunt. "To pretend."

"You'll see the real Lucky as much as

possible, I promise," said Auntie Jill.

Poppy gave her aunt a hug. "Thank you for getting him for me," she said.

When Uncle Simon came back with Lucky, Poppy gave him a hug too, and said, "Thank you so much, Uncle Simon."

He placed Lucky in her arms. "He's yours," he said. "So why don't you carry him back to the car?"

They had brought a box from home to put Lucky in for the journey. He didn't seem to mind going in it.

"He's a good boy," said Poppy proudly. "It'll be fun training him."

"Well, you can certainly help us with *that*!" said Uncle Simon.

All the way home Poppy couldn't stop talking to Lucky. When they got to Auntie Jill and Uncle Simon's house she couldn't wait to get him out of the box and cuddle him again.

"He's so cute!" she said, watching Lucky padding round the kitchen, sniffing everything and getting used to his new surroundings. "Shall we give him some water?"

"That's a good idea," agreed Auntie Jill. "Would you like to get it?"

They didn't have a dog bowl, so Poppy put some water in a baking dish and set it on the floor by the garden door. "He'll want to go out in the garden soon, won't he?" she asked, watching Lucky's pink tongue lapping the water.

"Definitely," said Auntie Jill. "His training starts here!"

The rain had stopped. Poppy, Auntie Jill and Lucky went into the garden, where the puppy dashed around, exploring everything. Although Poppy was wearing jeans and trainers, and the grass was wet, she was so happy she began to dance.

Auntie Jill came and joined her in the waltz. They danced round and round the garden, humming waltz music and giggling, and calling their pizza orders to Uncle Simon through the kitchen window. Lucky, beside himself with joy, ran in and out of their legs, almost tripping them over.

"He wants to dance too!" said Poppy. "Come on, Lucky, let me teach you the waltz!"

Uncle Simon had finished phoning for the

pizzas. He came into the garden and took over as Auntie Jill's partner, so that Poppy could pick up Lucky and dance with him in her arms. "This is so cool!" she exclaimed. "I thought today was going to be really boring. But it's been a brilliant, special Sunday!"

"It's not finished yet," said Auntie Jill. "Are you hungry?"

"I'm always hungry!" said Poppy, and she and Lucky went on dancing until the pizza arrived.

Fairy Godmother

It was the day of the Worthing Dance Workout.
Poppy knew that it wasn't a very important
competition in the world of ballroom dancing
as a whole, but in her small world of Brighton
and its nearby towns, it seemed just as
important as any other event she and Zack had
taken part in. And she was just as nervous.

"My legs are shaking!" she confessed to
Auntie Jill, who was pinning Poppy's hair up

into a bun, ready for her first dance.

"Everyone's nervous before a competition," said Auntie Jill, her words muffled because she was holding the hairpins between her lips. "But you know all your dances, don't you?"

Yes, Poppy did know all her dances, but that didn't help. All she could think about was that Miss Johnson had said that she and Zack were good enough to be among the winners. "If you win something before we all go up to Blackpool," she'd told them, "it'll boost your confidence."

"We're supposed to win," Poppy said to her aunt. "And that's scary."

Auntie Jill gave Poppy a quick hug. "Winning's not everything, you know," she said. "Dancing's about having fun as well. Now, where's Lucky?"

Lucky the soft toy, not the real puppy, was peeking out from Poppy's dance bag. "I'll hold him up and wiggle him while you're dancing," said Auntie Jill, "so he can see you."

"I'm not three years old!" Poppy said, giggling. She was glad her aunt had made her laugh, because it was hard to laugh *and* be nervous.

Just then a very excited-looking Zack appeared. "Guess what!" he said. "There's a special prize for the winners of each event – two free tickets to the Nationwide Finals in Blackpool, with everything paid for! Wouldn't it be great if we won that, Pop?"

Poppy and her aunt looked at each other. "But, Zack, everything's already organized," said Auntie Jill. "You and Poppy don't need the prize."

"But if we won it," said Zack eagerly, "we could give it to my Auntie Lynn, so she and my cousin Anna could come and watch us!"

"What a brilliant idea!" exclaimed Poppy.

It was time for the first round of the ballroom competition. "Dance well and enjoy yourselves," said Miss Johnson as Zack and Poppy walked onto the dance floor.

Poppy's new dress for Blackpool wasn't finished yet, so she was wearing her lemon-coloured dress and a matching ribbon in her hair. On her feet were white socks and new dancing shoes. Zack looked very smart in his black trousers, white shirt and lemon-coloured tie.

The Viennese waltz was an old-fashioned dance done to old-fashioned music that Poppy always

thought of as "oom-pa-pa"
music. The dancers turned and
turned around the room, first
one way, then the other, making
the dance look as lilting as the
music. "Keep smiling!" Poppy
reminded herself. "You never
know who's watching you!"

The judges walked around
the edge of the floor, watching each dancer
carefully, deciding which of them should
go through to the next round. Poppy could
feel that Zack was dancing his very best. He
really, really wanted to win that prize!

"Great!" said Miss Johnson when they
came off.

"Lucky says 'woof!'," added Auntie Jill,
"which means 'great!' in dog-speak."

"Oh, Auntie Jill, stop it!" exclaimed Poppy, though she couldn't help laughing. She was relieved that the first dance was over, and that they'd done it so well.

"Come on, Pop," said Zack, taking Poppy's hand. "It's the samba next. We'd better go and practise."

Poppy loved the Latin American dances, where the couples were free to dance apart as well as together, side by side, one in front of the other, or even back to back. She and Zack were good at the samba, a bouncy dance full of hip-swirling walks. Poppy saw the judges writing things on their notepads as she danced past. She hoped they were impressed.

In the next ballroom

round they did the foxtrot. Poppy knew that the judges would be looking for the correct dance hold, smooth steps and perfect timing in this slow, elegant dance.

"I bet you'll make the final!" said Auntie Jill, hugging them both. "And the next dance is your favourite, the jive. That's lucky!"

"Lucky's brought me luck!" Poppy exclaimed, kissing the top of the toy's head.

Poppy always had fun when she and Zack were kicking, turning and jumping in time to the toe-tapping jive music. They both put all their energy into doing the liveliest, bounciest jive possible. When they came off the floor they were breathless and hot, but very happy.

Miss Johnson was happy too. "If you don't get through to the finals," she said, "I'll eat my hat."

Poppy thought this was funny, especially as Miss Johnson never even wore a hat! But she wouldn't have had to eat it anyway. Poppy and Zack's numbers were announced for the ballroom final, and off they went to dance the quickstep.

It was a hard dance, full of quick steps as its name showed. Poppy and Zack had to move swiftly across the floor doing bouncing, tripping steps on the balls of their feet. Too much bouncing and it looked silly. But too little and it didn't look like a quickstep.

Zack was still trying hard. But to Poppy's dismay, he was trying a bit *too* hard. "It's not *jumping*," Miss Johnson had told them a hundred times. "You're not a couple of kangaroos." But Zack was definitely jumping.

Miss Johnson was still smiling when they came off the floor, but Poppy was sure that she had seen Zack's kangaroo steps. "Time to practise for the Latin final," she said. "It's the cha-cha-cha."

Poppy liked the swingy cha-cha-cha, with its little shuffle step that gave it a cheeky look. She and Zack were usually good at it. But today Poppy kept getting ahead of the beat. Perhaps, like Zack, she was trying too hard to win.

Everyone waited nervously as the results were announced. Ballroom was first. "In third place," said the announcer, "Poppy Love and Zack Bishop!"

Poppy and Zack ran to the table to collect the trophy for third place. As they posed for photographs, Poppy whispered to Zack, "Don't feel too bad."

"It's OK, Pop," he said. "I know I messed up that quickstep."

Poppy knew she'd messed up the cha-cha-cha, but didn't say so. Perhaps the judges hadn't noticed.

But they had. In the Latin competition, Poppy and Zack were placed second. Miss Johnson comforted them. "You danced really well all through, but just lost a bit of confidence in the final," she said.

Poppy felt like crying. "I wanted to win so that Anna and her mum could come to Blackpool!" she said to Auntie Jill. "And now they can't!"

"Shh," said Auntie Jill, cuddling her. "You did your very best."

Suddenly a voice said, "Are you Jill Jordan?"

"Yes," said Auntie Jill, turning round.

"Well, I was before I was married. I'm Jill Forrester now."

A fair-haired lady stood there smiling, holding a gold envelope. "I thought I recognized you," she said. "My name's Rosemary Smithson. I used to enjoy watching you so much when you were a dancer! You and your partner lit up the floor."

Auntie Jill still had her arm around Poppy. "Thank you," she said. "This is my niece, Poppy."

"I'm very pleased to meet you, Poppy," said Mrs Smithson. Then she held out the envelope towards Auntie Jill. "My grandson Toby came first in the ballroom section, and won these tickets," she explained. "But he won't be going to Blackpool this year because we're going to visit relatives in Australia at Easter. Would you like them instead?"

Poppy couldn't believe she had heard correctly. She and her aunt gasped with surprise. "Are you sure?" asked Auntie Jill.

Mrs Smithson nodded, looking across the room to a blond boy holding the first place trophy. "Toby says Poppy and her partner were so good, they deserve them."

"That's so kind of him!" said Auntie Jill. She turned to Poppy. "What do you think we should do?" she asked.

Poppy was still holding Lucky. This was better luck than he had ever brought her before. "I hope Anna can come to Blackpool!" she said, squeezing him tight.

"Who's Anna?" asked Mrs Smithson, interested.

"She's Zack's – my partner's – cousin,"
explained Poppy. "She loves dance, but she's
in a wheelchair."

"Then please give her these tickets with my
best wishes," said Mrs Smithson, putting the
envelope into Poppy's hand.

"Thank you!" cried Poppy. "Thank you so
much!"

While Auntie Jill thanked Mrs Smithson
too, Poppy waved to the blond boy. "Thank
you, Toby!" she called out, and he grinned
and waved back.

Poppy ran to tell Zack the news.

"Where have you been?" he asked before
she could speak. "You'd better get changed –
we're on in five minutes!"

In all the excitement Poppy had almost
forgotten about the Argentine tango show

dance. Cora, Sophie, Luke and Sam were already in their costumes, and Miss Johnson was holding out Poppy's dress. "Put this on, Poppy, and I'll fix the flowers in your hair," she said.

Poppy ran to the changing room, scrambled into the black dress with its shimmering red lining and fastened the choker round her neck. "Argentina, here I come!" she said to herself.

Miss Johnson fixed a red rose in the back of Poppy's dark hair. Then the trumpet, guitars and drums of the tango music began to play, and she forgot about everything except dancing.

Poppy still hadn't had a moment to tell Zack about Toby Smithson's generous gift, but she could see that he had put his disappointment behind him. He danced the Argentine tango better than ever before. On the step where the three girls leaned backwards, held by the boys, and trailed their hands along the floor, the crowd whistled and clapped. It was a hard move, but they'd done it perfectly.

"Let me hug all six of you!" said Miss Johnson happily when the dance was over.

The boys didn't much like being hugged, but they loved Miss Johnson and were glad she was pleased with their performance. "This has been a pretty good day after all!" said Zack.

"Oh, Zack!" cried Poppy, remembering. "I've got something to tell you!"

Zack and the others were astonished to hear about the gift of the tickets. "Wow!" exclaimed Zack, his eyes bright. "Wait till I tell my mum!"

Just then, Auntie Jill appeared. "When you've changed, shall we all get some drinks at the café?" she asked. "I've asked Mrs Smithson and Toby to join us."

Everyone was very excited as they gathered round the table in the café.

"Today's been like the Cinderella story," said Poppy, taking a sip of her strawberry milkshake. "Cinders couldn't go to the ball, just like Anna couldn't go to Blackpool. But then her Fairy Godmother came along and said, 'You *shall* go to the ball! Well, Blackpool.' Mrs Smithson must be Anna's Fairy Godmother!"

They all laughed. "Well," said Mrs
Smithson. "I've been a mother, and a
grandmother, and an ordinary godmother.
But I think being a Fairy Godmother is the
best job of all, thanks to you, Poppy Love!"

Natasha May loves dance of all kinds. When she was a little girl she dreamed of being a dancer, but also wanted to be a writer. "So writing about dancing is the best job in the world," she says. "And my daughter, who is a dancer, keeps me on my toes about the world of dance."

Shelagh McNicholas loves to draw people spinning around and dancing. Her passion began when her daughter, Molly, started baby ballet classes, "and as she perfected her dancing skills we would practise the jive, samba and quickstep all around the house!"